ONE
LEG
DANCING

by Cee McAdams

WingSpan Press

Published in the United States and the United Kingdom
by WingSpan Press, Livermore, CA

The WingSpan name, logo and colophon are the
trademarks of WingSpan Publishing.

ISBN 978-1-63683-076-6 (pbk.)
ISBN 978-1-63683-936-3 (ebk.)

First edition 2025

Printed in the United States of America
www.wingspanpress.com

Other Books by Cee McAdams:

LOW HANGING BRANCHES
(temporarily out of print)

CLOUD COVER

QUARTER MOON MYSTERIES

JOURNEY

DON'T LOOK BACK

IN THE GARDEN OF MOONLIGHT

DON'T STAY TOO LONG BY THE RIVER

"THESE BOOTS ARE MADE FOR
BUTT KICKING."

Kalen Chapman Lloyd

ONE LEG DANCING

(Introduction)

Ona Louise was an emotionally distraught woman...she had lost everyone she loved and everyone who mattered to her: Ben, her husband of 24 years, her daughter, her son-in-law...even her rescued cat deserted her...she just wanted to live long enough to get into her favorite chair and die in peace.

A few months ago, she met someone who changed all of that...she refers to him only as 'Lom.' Since then, she no longer wakes up with tears on her cheeks, but instead, she has a song in her heart and a smile on her face. She has begun to believe that the lonely days are over and that hope, love and laughter will consume the rest of her life. Ona Louise is once again a happy woman with new horizons to pursue...she has Lom and her little grandson, Jan-Mikel Traenor, whom she affectionately calls 'Yanny.'

She has raised 'Yanny' since he was 19 months, (he is now 18) after an out-of-control driver of an 18-wheeler ran a red light and took his parents away from him and away from Ona Louise.

But all is not well...Ben, her late husband, had 2 daughters from his first marriage and they are planning to make life not only miserable for Ona Louise but leave her penniless and homeless as well...they believe that their father should have left all of his worldly possessions to them, which could not be farther from the truth...they deserted him when he was ill and needed them, while Ona Louise stayed by his side until the end. His will was very specific: they would get not a dime...they have contested the will to no avail, threatened to put the grandson out of his home, took a shot at her but only injured her and thankfully not too seriously...there is no way of knowing what they will do next...the time has come – in the midst of her fears, she will have to fortify her resolve and be prepared for anything...she cannot afford to wait to see if they will get on with their lives and leave her to hers.

What Ona Louise cannot know is that during these moments of dark reverie, during her waking hours as well as when she has been plagued by insomnia, there is a force afoot. For Metropolis, there was Superman...for Century City, there was the Green Hornet...Southern California had El Zorro – but Ona Louise has El Vengador... only those who wish to cause her harm, specifically Wynne and Renotta, will learn of his existence.

ONE LEG DANCING

The pain and agony of losing a child is beyond indescribable...it squeezes your heart...it takes not only your breath away but your will to live. Everywhere you go, in every little corner, you see something that reminds you of her...even a flower garden where there is a bloom that she liked or a hummingbird which she adored, will set you once again spinning into a fit of misery. I tell myself that I will get over it and find peace but this is harder than you can possibly imagine. Some days, I feel as if I've been sent to a dark place where there is not enough oxygen, where I have to fight for each breath. With each passing day, I fear that I will lose my mind from grief too heavy to bear, but fear and grief are conspiring to make me an emotional wreck...I will not allow this to happen...I've got too much to live for. Whenever these moments of dark reverie threaten to take control of my day, I have to fight my way through them...on warm and sunny days, I put on my walking shoes and just walk through the park for an hour or so...I gaze at the azaleas and breathe in the fragrant breezes from the jasmine... by the time I make it back to my house, the sick heavy feeling around my heart has evaporated and a brighter mood floats to the top.

I don't remember falling asleep, just a lot of tossing and chasing after my blanket... something kept pulling it off and my feet kept feeling exposed, but I awoke to a gloriously warm and sunny day...I called Lom and told him that we should plan a picnic at the place where water seeps through the rocks and the sky seem to go on for miles, clear and blue....we call it our own little waterfall. He tells me that he will bring the wine and his own fork.

☽

I find a basket and fill it with grapes, cheeses, pate', bottled water, eclairs, spicy pickles, glasses and napkins. Our favorite blanket is still in Lom's truck from our last outing so I remind him to gather it up and make sure that it's clean and free from whatever he may have tossed in his truck on top of it...then I lock all of my doors, make sure there are no windows left open and off I go...I will leave my vehicle in his garage because our picnic spot is closer to his house than mine. He is waiting for me at the front porch with a long stem rose in one hand and wearing the world's biggest smile!

Lom, which of course is not his real name, but it works for me and he doesn't mind the moniker...he is tall, a bit on the husky side but nowhere near fat...he has shoulders as wide as a B1, a broad chest that seems to always be pushing against his shirt...with his regal bearing, sexy is not a word that would be comfortable for him but dapper hardly begins to cover it...thankfully, he is beyond the age of wanting to wear tight jeans but he always looks ravishing nevertheless.

One Leg Dancing

I drove across town with the breezes in my hair and a song in my heart...I pulled into Lom's driveway, stepped out of the car and we embraced like old lovers...while we are transferring the basket of food from my vehicle to his, my mood suddenly darkens...we are about to have visitors. My body goes rigid as I look around for a weapon. Seeing nothing suitable, I simply back up against Lom and wait to see what happens next....I didn't have long to wait... trouble has arrived.

It's a little hard to think of these two as being real women let alone having been the offspring of my now deceased husband Ben...Wynne, the older one, has the personality of a rhubarb, is built like a port-a-potty and has a mouth to match... Renotta, the younger one is so intellectually anemic that she basically has only a sliver of a personality...her sister does her thinking and everything else for her except her bathroom visits. Now they have graced us with their presence and destroyed what was meant to be a totally beautiful day!

Wynne jumps out of the car and comes at me like some highly disturbed simian creature...I stand my ground...her face darkens and her mouth opens and closes like a bass out of water but no words come out...she seems torn between flying into a rage and sitting on the ground and crying like a child...but she does neither one of these things...instead, she saunters up to Lom and asked him to leave us while we have a private chat...Lom stands where he is and looks her in the eye...she makes a fist and then releases it...her eyes opens and closes several times as she grows more and more enraged. She decides that he is neither intimated nor is he amused with any of her antics so she sends me a lightening strike of a look...Lom moves over a step closer to me...I can feel his body tense and the wind shift only slightly...this seemed to infuriate her more and made her even more frustrated...she makes balled up fists once again and finally, she backs up, says words I could not understand but no doubt words one would not use in church, and moments later, they are back in their vehicle and driving away...her younger sister never said one word...I wanted to comment but words seemed totally inadequate. Our picnic all but forgotten, Lum collects our basket and we move back inside the house.

I'm a bit shaken by this encounter but I'm trying not to show it...Lom has noticed me rubbing my chest ever so slightly as if there is a tiny insect in there trying to find his way out...I find a chair the farthest away from the door and plop down as if I weigh a ton...Lom is observing but says nothing at first and then he offers to spread the blanket in the backyard so we can still have our picnic...I decline but instead suggested that we have our   lunch inside, that I could

chill the wine and make a nice salad...I don't tell him that I've got a lump in my throat and that it would be a little difficult to swallow the cheese. This is going to have to end... this thought has intruded on my day again and again...I cannot allow these two women to continue to disrupt my life just because it pleases them. I express my frustration to Lom, then head for the kitchen to start lunch...I pour us each a glass of un-chilled wine...Lom makes no comment.

The problem with these two women began long before Lom came into my life... it, in all likelihood, began at birth but that would be unfair to their mother. I can no longer recall any details about her as a person or what kind of life they may have had together...it was many years after her death that I married Ben and over the years he would only mention something about their history in passing. I believe these daughters became obsessed with having me out of his life when they learned that he had left a will...they did not have access to the contents which drove them mad. Wynne, the older of the two, tried everything to force me to provide evidence that Ben left everything to them, which not only was not true, but I refused to be intimidated.

As his health further declined, he would call them simply because he wanted the comfort of having his children around... there was always a problem and they would not show up, even when they promised him that they would...the very last thing he told me was that they were not to get a dime, but if worse became worst, that there was an old house [he had acquired in a shady deal] that I could allow them to live in, but only if it meant they would be otherwise homeless and out on the street. Even though I could not have known this at the time, his near prediction was about to become reality... worse was about to rear its ugly head.

According to the cryptic messages Wynne leaves me on my voicemail, she and her sister are having serious financial difficulties and need money badly... she screams into my phone that it is my fault and that I should move out of my home and give it to them since they are the rightful heirs...I can only imagine her balling up her fist and wanting to punch through the cyber walls to make her point.

Some days I'm simply overcome with grief and can hardly get through the day, but on this beautiful day, with not a cloud in sky, when he was out of class and had a few minutes to spare, I went over for a short visit with my grandson Yanny. He is fond of blueberry muffins and I sometimes use these like weapons to get his time and attention...I would never confess that I am lonely and needed to hug him as if it will give me much needed oxygen. He has been told of the tragic loss of his parents but always calls me Mama because I'm the only one he knows...he was only an infant when his mother was taken away from him but I suppose he remembers her on a level that I cannot possibly understand.

We enjoy our muffins and lemonade and chat about nothing in particular, just the sound of his voice is like a magic elixir for my troubled spirit and soothes my soul. He is a bright and energetic child and knows nothing of the trouble I'm having with those daughters of Ben...he only sees them as odd and 'sort of' family but has no real connection and certainly no relationship with either one of them.

Our chat and muffins end much too soon but I can think of no other reasons to keep him from his activities, so I pick up my muffin dish and head for home. As I'm pulling into my driveway, I get the strange feeling that I am being watched or rather that I'm about to drive into a storm unseen just around the corner of my driveway. I move forward slowly but see nothing...I take my eyes off the driveway for only a nanosecond and reach for my remote...when I look up, I think I saw a shadow but insisted that it was only my imagination...I hit the remote, pull into the garage and I'm about to step out of my car when suddenly she is there pointing a gun at me...she fires, striking me in the ankle. I close the door and slam the car into reverse before I think about what to do next. I'm seized with rage at the fact that she is trespassing on my property and has shot and wounded me in the process.

I speed down the street in the general direction of the medical center but I'm in unbelievable pain...I can hardly steer and I know I'm bleeding all over the floor of my car...I realize that I'm not going to make it to the medical center so I go directly to a stand-alone minor emergency clinic not far from my house. I stop the engine and drag myself out of the car and barely make it to the door before I pass out.

When I'm conscious again, I realize that nearly two hours have passed...I send Lom a text message to let him know where I am but told him not to alert my grandson...I don't want to worry him. Instead of responding with a text message, he calls and wants details...I explain as best I can but fear I must have imagined it all. The nurses have bandaged my leg – the bullet went in and out just above my ankle and apparently caused no permanent damage except for the scar that will surely last the rest of my life, as a bitter reminder. Lom informs me that he is coming to drive me home but I insist that I can make it since I have been supplied with pain killers and it's only a short drive to the house...I would, however, really appreciate his company and a little surveillance.

We arrive back at my house and make it inside without further incident...it gives me such a feeling of serenity to know that Lom is close...he gets me set up in a comfortable chair and with a pillow for my foot. I think that only the pain meds are keeping me from shaking like a leaf in a strong wind... this has shaken me to my core.

Wynne drives like Lucifer himself is chasing her, so pleased is she with herself that she has pulled of this minor crime wave all by herself and has gotten away freely. She is trembling with excitement and pleads with herself to calm down...she sets her bag down on the sofa and goes over to the sink in the kitchen to splash cold water on her face...this done, she reaches for a paper towel and happens to glance out of the window...there she notices someone standing in the shadow of the weeds and grass in the overgrown yard...upon closer inspection, she discovers that it is not someone but a something, since she can see only one leg...suddenly it moves lightning-fast and is right behind her before she can move out of her tracks...attached to this leg is a large fierce-looking boot with a pointed toe and it aims an amazingly powerful kick at her left leg...before she can turn to face it, the boot unleashed another one at her left knee and she crumples to the floor...she sat there screaming in pain but no one can hear her...her sister is not home and there is no one else to come to her rescue. She loses conscientiousness and El Vengador left the house the same way he entered... silently.

When she wakes up, her sister is standing

over her, perspiring profusely as if she has fallen in the pool, and looking terrified... Wynne is hurt, her leg and her knee are both badly swollen but she will live...unfortunately, she will be walking with a slight limp for a few weeks...her sister Renotta is asking a million questions but Wynne is too afraid of sounding demented to answer any of them... how will she explain that a disembodied boot, not a person, did this to her... worse still, her excitement of wounding Ona Louise earlier has totally deflated and has been replaced with a sense of fear that is threatening to immobilize her...she cannot afford to become hysterical... she has to find a way out her dilemma...she has lost her job and her lease and is about to be evicted unless she can convince or persuade Ona Louise to give her enough money to see her through this nightmare...otherwise, she will have to continue to terrorize Ona Louise until she agrees to move out of the house left by their father so that she and her sister will have a place to live...she does not believe in ghosts or spirits so how will she ever explain this boot, IF that is indeed what she saw.

She and her sister are running out of time...the only thing they can do at the moment is to begin packing up their belongings and be ready for whatever comes next. Wynne decided that she would take another crack at Ona Louise but she would wait until her leg didn't hurt so much and only then she would wait until it was near dark when she knew Ona Louise would be alone...another face to face should do it, when her tall friend was not around...she knew that Ona Louise was hurt but had no clue just how badly... since it was in the lower leg, probably not too badly...not the shot she had intended, her aim was off so not good enough to convince her that Wynne was serious... that is going to require more and better planning. She is about to be thrown out in the street and this woman is in the house that is rightfully hers.

One Leg Dancing

Our 'acquired' house was hardly in a bucolic locale...it was an older house just north of ramshackle, in an old neighborhood where houses tend to get rundown and or simply not updated, and many times all but abandoned because the newer generation don't want the responsibility of remodeling them and won't live there otherwise... Ben told me that on a few occasions, the previous occupants had wild parties and that fights would break out over something as mundane as a spilled drink... although no one was ever charged because it was never proven, a guy whose name was "Cashew"... no one ever knew his real name...was killed in that house...the incident was covered up, the people involved disappeared and nothing ever came of it. The owner had tried for years to sell it but to no avail... out of desperation, he bartered with Ben to exchange it for a truck & trailer, neither was in very good condition...Ben gave him a few dollars just to ease his conscience, so the deal was struck and we neither saw nor heard from him again...we or rather I am now the proud owner of this house where this alleged death occurred, where the tenants heard alleged eerie whispers and soon I will hear of the alleged sound of non-existent dishes breaking and other such weird noises.

Over the years, Ben did manage to lease it a couple of times, but always people complained about their sleep being interrupted with strange sounds, like dishes breaking or stuff falling off the shelves... not a shred of tangible evidence was ever found but the noises would persist. After Ben was gone, I leased it again and heard all manner of wild stories from the tenants, from something skittering across the floor to water running to kitchen pots being scraped...I told them it was probably just clanging pipes since it was a rather old house or perhaps it was a small animal in the attic...they insisted that no animal made those sounds and invited me to stay the night so that I could witness these mysterious happenings myself... needless to say, I was skeptical, but I declined their invitation to stay the night...I did, however go over to investigate once or twice but found nothing amiss. In order to rid myself of any doubt that things were living in the walls or furniture, I had the place professionally cleaned, freshly painted and the old furniture moved out and replaced with new twin beds and new bedding plus a sofa and 2 chairs...after that, the tenants were satisfied for a while and then the complaints began again...they would tell me of lights going on and off in unoccupied rooms and of doors being slammed shut even though they had closed and/or locked the doors, that the noises would be louder and more persistent around midnight...they would search the entire house but always come away feeling ridiculous because nothing or no one was ever found...they finally gave up trying to convince me and themselves that the house was haunted or otherwise occupied or 'something' and they moved out after about a year...the place has been vacant ever since, for at least 4 years, or so I thought...the house was apparently still occupied.

Although Wynne and Renotta have packed up all of their belongings, they have no clue where they will go...her bruises have healed somewhat so she is able to walk and drive without too much pain...she decided that today is the day that she should make her final appeal to Ona Louise, with or without the aid of violence...today she is feeling empowered...the voices that she has heard before are back and telling her that she is right to fight for her inheritance. She believes in the voices...she knows nothing about psychology and that in all likelihood, she is experiencing symptoms of schizophrenia or some other form of mental impairment...she has never told anyone about hearing the voices because she only hears them at night when she is alone... sometimes the voices keep her awake most of the night giving her instructions on how to deal with those who wish to keep her from getting what is rightfully hers. The voices are quiet now so she takes this as a good sign that she is ready.

She awoke bright and cheerful, having slept through the night without hearing the sounds of the storm...it is overcast, not exactly pouring but a heavy drizzle is falling.... she can feel that the weather is beginning to darken her mood but only slightly...it is also later than she thinks and she has to plan her attack on Ona Louise...she has only one more night to be in this house before she and her sister will be without an address... just thinking about having to sit out in the rain while Ona Louise is inside the nice cozy home that should be hers, made her rage once again boil to nearly overflowing, but she feels warmed by cold hatred.

Wynne climbs out of bed, goes into the bathroom to splash water on her face to chase away the last vestiges of sleep, then she goes into the kitchen...without realizing it, she gazes out the window, still thinking about her encounter with the boot...she has decided that in her emotional state, that she obviously fell and hurt her knee and simply imagined the entire boot incident, that this is the only natural explanation... it could not have materialized, caused her harm and then simply disappeared like a puff of smoke...so why is she looking out of the window expecting to see it? She's not totally convinced that her explanation is good enough.

Wynne has decided to enlist the help of her sister on this 3-step mission of coaxing Ona Louise to leave her house...first, she will make sure that her tall friend is not around... then she will get Renotta to stand guard to make sure they are not disturbed, and finally to alert her if anyone shows up...she wants no interference while she is having her chat with Ona Louise, although chat is not exactly what she has in mind.

Around 5 in the evening, the rain has all but stopped and Wynne thinks the time is right...they sat in Ona Louise's driveway for about 10 minutes, just having a look around and listening to the wind sing in the trees. Finally, she gets out, walks up to the door and rings the doorbell. When the door is opened, much to her surprise, she is invited in, offered a cup of tea and told to make herself comfortable...this was not part of the plan so Wynne was momentarily flummoxed and nearly spilled her tea...she recovered immediately and forced herself to stay on track.

They sat in the den, not exactly chatting like old friends...Ona Louise is explaining that she has listened to the voicemail messages and that she sympathizes with her financial plight...the fact remains, she is stating patiently, that you and your sister were both left out of your father's will as you already know, and would get neither property or funds...she continues to explain that there does exist a house which she would consider allowing them to live in under certain conditions. Wynne began to shake her head so violently that this time she did indeed spill her tea...she sprang to her feet and shouted at Ona Louise that she had no intentions of living anyplace other than the house where she was currently standing and that was that. She turned and headed for the door but only made it part of the way before she encountered or sensed a fast-moving shadow that struck her with such force that it knocked her to her hands and knees...she looked around but saw nothing...she struggled, finally made it back to standing then limped out of the door as fast as she could and climbed into her car.

Wynne tried to rationalize what had just happened but soon accepted that it was beyond her ability to understand... something certainly attacked her – she had a bright new bruise as proof...Renotta was staring at her wide-eyed but Wynne pretended not to notice, just started the car and backed out of the driveway. Ona Louise was standing in the door and waved a friendly goodbye as they drove away. Once they were back at the house where they have been evicted, she told her sister of the offer from Ona Louise...her sister looked puzzled but thought that perhaps her offer was not as bad as it sounds...besides, they had no place else to go.

One Leg Dancing

And so, it was settled...the next day, bright and early, they would drive to this place and have a look at this house which may very well be their new forever home. They will soon find out that peaceful appearances can sometimes be deceiving.

BLATTODEA MANOR

When Wynne and Renotta arrived at the house, they were at first somewhat pleasantly surprised and then Wynne was almost immediately seized with a feeling of foreboding; the house appeared to be large, about 3 bedrooms, with a back porch and a covered patio...there was very little grass but they decided that that would not be much of a problem since neither of them had a hankering to do lawn work. Ona Louise had given her instructions on how to find the keys...she should go inside the shed in back, look underneath an old upside down rusted can, and there she will find the keys...she followed the path to the door of the shed, with her sister right on her heels, pulled on the door which groaned like an animal in great pain, but finally it came open...there was no light switch inside that she could find so Renotta held the door wide open to let in as much light as possible. After stepping over several pieces of broken tools and assorted bugs and small animals, she was able to find the shelf where there was an upside-down can...she lifted it carefully and underneath, she found the keys...and a very large cockroach. With her heart pounding, she rushed out and quickly closed the shed door.

Renotta, being the squeamish one, refused to go inside first...she didn't even want to go inside second...there were spider's webs everywhere...a large trapdoor spider had built an impressive web across the entrance to the kitchen, between the den and the kitchen and he was standing guard.

The house smelled like a combination of spilled beer, sweaty shoes, old grease, backed-up plumbing and rotting potatoes...it hardly looked lavish but it mostly just felt abandoned and unlived-in...otherwise, it looked like a lot of work just to get it clean enough to sleep in...but first, a tour.

By the end of the day, Wynne and Renotta had the floor mopped, the kitchen cleaned and their clothes hung in their respective closets...there were two small bathrooms so they each had a bathroom to herself. The beds were small, twin size, but neither complained nor did either give the slightest thought to leaving...this was going to have to be home unless fortune smiled on them, and that hardly seemed likely since they had been left out of their father's will without a dime. Now though, they would have to go to the grocery store and buy what they could...Wynne had no job but neither did she have rent to pay...Renotta had very little money...Wynne would have to find a job very soon so that she could pay her share.

They were so exhausted from cleaning and making the house livable that they just wanted to sleep for a week and then finish the unpacking, so when the nightly noises started, neither was the wiser. It was only the persistent scratching at her window that finally awakened Wynne with a sudden jolt of fear. She sat up and looked around but saw nothing...she told herself that it was a case of the jitters from being in an old unfamiliar house the first night...her nerves jangled but she convinced herself that's all it was, jangled nerves...she could not have been more wrong.

In addition to what the past tenants would have me believe were restless spirits,

there were other forces running loose in the house. The former owners were not very tidy and neither were any of the subsequent tenants...they would drink to excess and leave partially eaten sandwiches or sometimes nearly a full plate of food untouched and uncovered...this was an invitation too good to pass up for a certain species of uninvited guests. Even though I did have the place cleaned at one point, I did not repeat this chore before Wynne and her sister moved in...this was one of the conditions, that they would be responsible for the cleaning, as well as activating the utilities. I would subsequently learn that the six-legged inhabitants had taken a stand and had no intention of leaving, since they had been there first and had been there longer than anyone else...they were prepared to stand their ground...Wynne and Renotta were about to cross swords with both the seen and the unseen.

Another day of looking around the nest and seeing nothing...it's getting so that whether hunting night or day, it produces nothing but more disappointment and empty bellies. Our new landlord is determined to drive us out or starve us out and we have got to come up with a better way to feed ourselves or we will not survive, let alone reproduce and prosper.

Belle, the Blattodea matriarch, was at it again, prancing around twitching and ranting about there being no food.

One Leg Dancing

"Grubbe," she yelled..."why can't you be a better hunter? There has to be some provisions that you're missing...don't look in the usual places...we cannot depend on living on leftovers alone...we've got to be clever and do the unexpected...let's contact Crocus...he'll know what to do."

Crocus is enormous, almost 3 times as big as the rest of us...he would grind and grit and twitch and little spasms would pass through us. Crocus is a rambler, sometimes traveling over great distances. He has been around a long time and has survived 2 owners and 3 renters...in those days, we never had to worry about food...there was always plenty, a literal banquet day or night. Crocus and the boys would have their fill and then bring back enough to last in case pickings were slim the next night...of course they never were, not until now... in these desperate times, we need Crocus.

Crocus' first duty was to take a look around, a little lite reconnaissance to check things out, get the lay of the land and then, if necessary, call in re-enforcements. The first night produced nothing. Crocus came back with empty pockets and an empty belly, nothing to eat or drink, just thoughts of smells of food that was no longer there... no good news to report...this went on for weeks until finally Crocus hit the jackpot...or so he thought.

Crocus was making his nightly rounds a bit earlier than usual in an area where he didn't normally go when the smell of something pungent nearly knocked him over. Reluctantly he eased over to the crack in the door and took a sniff...the smell made him woozy with excitement and anticipation. He had been hungry for so long that his insides were beyond empty. He peered around the corner and lurched slightly sideways as the sight of all that red deliciousness nearly overwhelmed him. 'This is no time for caution,' he chided himself... no furtive glances or sneaky looks, just go for it, but first better signal for the troops... this might be the big one.

The first to arrive was old Flattop, rushing across the floor as if he was already late for work. The next ones were Crud and Pudgy and then so many others. Crocus was in front, proudly leading the pack but was so focused on what was ahead that he failed to see that huge wave of doom named Wynne coming straight for him. The impact was horrific...Crocus didn't have time to take evasive action...he was done for, 'deader' than dead, his last thoughts were that he never got to enjoy that fantastic feast, nor did the rest of them realize that their joy would be short-lived as well and that soon they would be on their way to join Crocus.

They all rushed over and dived into what looked like a tower of the most tantalizing treat ever...they stuffed themselves, packed up as much as they could carry but didn't make it very far before they fell into a deep sleep from which none of them would ever awaken, not from a bite of the poison apple but a taste of a double-doctored tomato.

Belle was in a tizzy, pacing back and forth, twitching and muttering to whomever

happened to be close by but mostly to herself...Grubbe, Crocus nor any of the others had come back...she had sent out searchers but they had not returned either... she needed to get them all together so that they could plot their revenge...the oleic was really strong and she was certain that her worse fears had been realized, that they had incurred the wrath of the current tenants and that all of them were dead.

Wynne and Renotta had never seen so many large cockroaches and one such extremely large one...they didn't know if they should call the exterminator or throw a saddle on it...he was not only nearly as large as a Shetland but bold as brass...in fact, none of them would try to run and hide in dark corners but they stood their ground as if daring Wynne to attack them. Quickly she realized that she was in for a fight. By sheer carelessness, she had left a tomato out on the counter and only remembered when she went into the kitchen for a glass of water before bedtime...this had given her an idea.

She had found 2 different kinds of poison in the shed so she went out to collect about a tablespoon full to mix in the tomato that she could no longer eat anyway. She carefully opened the top and poured in the entire large spoonful and then left it siting where it was. The next morning, much to her delight, there were several of them lying nearby, after sampling the midnight snack she had left for them...they were going to have a very long sleepover...sometimes you really can't go home again...score one for Wynne.

The previous night Wynne and Renotta had talked about their new abode, that it was not nearly as bleak as Ona Louis had made it sound, especially after the cleaning and the new curtains...Renotta commented about hearing sounds but decided that it was nothing or just the wind welcoming them to their new castle...Wynne had heard strange sounds as well but was not so sure

it was the wind but thought it was certainly something speaking to her, only it was not a welcome message. She decided to ignore it for the moment and try to get a good night's sleep...tomorrow, she would go out and look for a job.

I have been relatively silent since the arrival of the new tenants or whatever they might be, but now I think it's time they feel my presence. Cashew, a handle I acquired as a little boy because I loved them more than anything else...they were always on my mom's grocery list along with the other food essentials...I could live without chips, jellybeans or football, but not cashews...you may have known me in my previous state of existence but you may not want to know me at all in my present state of 'non-existence', not that it really matters since nothing causes me any concern or confusion or gives me any reason to worry about anything at all...I did come to the conclusion that after the long years of roaming the house in relative peace, that now I will have to go back to making the occupants feel as unwanted as I have felt for many years...I was tossed aside and left in a heap on the floor as if I mattered not at all.

As my former self, I worked on a construction crew...several of the guys would get together on weekends and play poker, drink beer and have a few laughs, just to chill and unwind from the week of hard work...one night the party took a wrong turn...one guy, who was an especially bad loser, thought he had been cheated... the more some of the other guys tried to reason with him, the louder and angrier he became...of course he had had one beer too many so he was beyond reason... he began waving a large caliber handgun around and finally pointed it at the person whom he believed had wronged him...I stepped between them with the intention of disarming him by knocking the gun to the floor but he shot me instead...much to my disbelief and horror, no one called 911...

after a minute or two, most of the guys fled the scene...the guy who lived there and one other guy, found an old blanket which they threw over me, that had not seen any detergent for many years...they were at first undecided as to what to do with me, but the owner finally made the decision to take me out to the construction site, afraid that if the authorities found out what had happened in the house, they would all lose their jobs or worse...they hauled me away and dumped me in that construction site, then covered me over and no one was ever the wiser...unknow to them, only the outer shell was tossed away like so much garbage...the other part of me never left the house.

I have been unable to rest in peace and neither will anyone else...my family never knew what happened to me...they have lived with the idea that I simply vanished without a trace...at first, they insisted that we had all been part of the same crew but inquiries came back empty so law enforcement authorities had no clues to follow, nothing to go on...it didn't take long for the matter to become of no further concern and the case, such as it was, was closed. Now others have to know that I am still where they discarded me, only not in the same condition or the same form...sometimes I'm a shadow, sometimes I'm a whisper or a broken dish or a gust of wind...sometimes I unleash sadistic attacks and other times I'm almost playful in my choice of antics...sometimes I'm the sound of your heart constricting but always I'm an irrational uncomprehending presence.

Wynne came awake with a start, not sure what had awakened her...she immediately felt a strange draft, a smell she couldn't quite describe...as she looked around, her confusion deepened...this was not the same room where she had fallen asleep, or it at least didn't look or feel quite the same...the window was open and she was certain that she had closed it before going to sleep...she stood on wabbly legs and made her way to the closet intending to reach for her bathrobe but found the bathrobe on the chair along with most of her other clothes...fear was beginning to creep into every pore, making her hands shake and her head throb...she needed to go and check on her sister but realized that Renotta would have already left for work... she decided to go to her room anyway, just to check, just in case.

She found Renotta's room empty and her bed neatly made...nothing seemed out of place so she walked through the rest of the house but found nothing amiss...her fear slowly subsided as she headed for the kitchen to make herself breakfast before venturing out to look for work. As she turned the corner, she was met with a smack across the face by something damp, the size of a bath towel and smelling of kerosene...an icy chill roared up her spine as she struggled to reach the sofa before she lost her balance... even over the cacophony of her racing heart and her silent screams, she could hear the sound of unearthly laughter. Fear again wrapped itself around her heart and left her gasping for breath.

Fearing that she was losing her mind, she wanted to get out of the house but first she wanted to call Ona Louise...that thought died before it could take root in her mind, certain she would tell her that she was hallucinating or worse, order her to vacate the house, then she and her sister would again be without a place to stay...she had no one else to call...maybe just step outside for a bit of fresh air and a new perspective.

Her heart thudded in her chest but slowly the racing became a crawl...she found herself whimpering, mumbling in total disbelief... where were those reassuring voices when she needed them? Did something just attach her in the kitchen? This time she checked herself and had no bruises, just a damp face...did she imagine it all? The smell of kerosene lingered.

Job hunting temporarily forgotten, Wynne ventured back into the house after about thirty minutes of listening to her blood pressure return to normal...slowly she re-entered her room and looked around...no clothes were on the chair...the window was closed and her bathrobe was just where she had left it the previous night. She really wanted to talk to Ona Louise if for no other reason than to hear another human voice, but also to tell her about these strange happenings...she could say how awful she felt for all of the nasty things she had said and done to her, especially for injuring her, for terrorizing her grandson, and for leaving rude messages on her voicemail...but she did not make the call... she was feeling lost and vulnerable, even felt a bit of remorse but not enough to apologize...she still felt that she should be in the house where Ona Louise lives and not in this place where she is under attack, even though she has serious doubts that any of it actually happened. She wanted to summon the voices so they could tell her what to do, but she had never summoned them before – they always came to her unbidden....she decided instead, that she would make herself some breakfast and wait until her sister made it home...on

One Leg Dancing

Saturday, Renotta will not have to go to work so they will have the entire weekend to come up with a plan.

Cashew decided that he was being too subtle...he would have to become more direct and bombard these women with his full arsenal of home-wrecking and sleep-deprivation activities...there were old bottles and a few cans left behind by previous tenants that he could toss but maybe a sub rosa visit with the younger one would do the trick...wait until she is just falling asleep and then manifest himself as her sister, only leave his head in another room...spectral but effective.

Renotta was getting ready for bed and singing quietly to herself...she was looking forward to Saturday so that she could have time to spend with her sister...Wynne had said that they needed to make some new plans but she could not imagine what they would plan to do...besides, Wynne was the smart one...whatever it is she is planning, I just know it will be fun.

Renotta turned out the light so the room was mostly bathed in darkness... the only light was from the moonlight filtered through the thin curtains...I waited and watched until she seemed to be comfortable and about to drift off to sleep...the chair was sitting at an odd angle to the foot of her bed and she was turned away with her back to me...I stumbled into the chair and made as much noise as I could...she turned over to have a look but I appeared to be only a shadow...she was trying to decide if I was a feminine figure sitting in her chair or just a figment of her imagination...deciding on the latter, she turned over and went still again...I moved the chair closer to the bed by scraping it across the floor...this brought her up with a start and a shriek...she stared at the chair wild-eyed and then all the light went out of eyes and she passed out.

When she awoke the following morning, with the incomprehensible image still fresh in her mind, Renotta ran into her sister's room to tell her all about it, only her words were tumbling all over themselves and she was all but incoherent. Wynne was intrigued by her story and could hardly wait to see if the chair was still occupied or if this was another of those inexplainable and mysterious episodes...she found the chair against the wall in its usual spot and there was nothing or no one sitting in it.

It's a strange contrast to being in the house alone and having other people moving around and making noises... the sound of music is not too bad but the sound of running water is especially annoying and it seems to take place in the evening or early hours of the night when they are getting ready for bed...I've had enough! I've decided that this is when I will speak to the older one...I will knock on her door and politely glide in...I know that she has a weapon, a gun which she has often left lying on her bedside table...I will of course remove the gun to make her feel just a bit off center, not because I fear she will injure me, which of course is quite impossible.

I have no way of knowing about the upbringing of these two women...they may have been taught that there is no such thing as spirits, sometimes referred to as ghosts...it is now my unpleasant task to show these two that there is still something to learn, even at this stage of their lives. First I will speak to the one named Wynne and tell her not to be afraid, which of course will chill her to her bones...I think it only fitting that I should appear to her as her sister since her sister was given the treat of seeing me as her the night before... she will be quite unprepared to deal with an unknown entity who appears to be her sister but with the head missing...I believe that her heart is strong enough so I will leave her no choice, so as soon as she turns out the light, I will make my entrance.

I knocked softly at first...when she did not respond, I knocked a bit louder... this time she asked me to enter...I swept into the room and pulled the only chair up close to her bed...her eyes widen in shock and total disbelief but I spoke softly to her and told her not to fear...this did nothing to calm her and she began to perspire heavily and moan quietly...the room felt stuffy so I opened the window to allow in some evening breezes and just a sliver of moonlight...the animals and insect sounds went silent immediately...I told her to think of me as another roommate and that she has nothing to fear, as long as we are mutually satisfied with the arrangement.

She starred at me, the only part that she could see but she was as pale as the proverbial ghost...I could see her thoughts churning but she did not make a sound other than the soft moans and beads of sweat popping out like small water balloons. I explained to her that if she and her sister would not run water late at night, that we could get along just fine...I have been here for a long time and I have no plans to leave, so we can either reach an agreement or you and your sister can find another place to stay. I give you my word that I will cause you no more nightmares and never again interrupt your sleep...of course if you do not agree, then you will never have another peaceful night, or day for that matter. I will now leave you to think it over. With that done, I closed the window, took my leave and the peaceful sounds of the night returned.

At first, Wynne did not understand what she had just seen, or rather she did not believe what she had just seen...she thought it best to tell herself that she had seen nothing out of the ordinary and certainly could not have heard from someone who wasn't there, then slowly realization dawned like a new day...she tried to stick her head out of the window that she thought had been open only a moment ago but found it closed...she wanted to hear the sound of the owls dispersing their wisdom, the chirp of the crickets, the buzzing of the cicadas other nightly noises so that she would know that all was right with the world...her world was not alright at all...she turned around and looked at her chair which was quite empty and not near her bed as it had been only moments before...she lay back on her bed and screwed her eyes tightly shut so that the tears would not flow...she made herself accept that she has been under a great deal of stress, losing her father who left her out of his will, losing her job and then losing the nice place where she and her sister had lived comfortably for so long...she thought about the things she had done and thought maybe the conscience that she had abandoned long ago, had just paid her a visit. A chilling thought but it has to be a better explanation than a headless female who otherwise resembled Renotta, had just tried to make a deal with her... another thought occurred to her: maybe she was crazy and had been for a long time...there had certainly been other signs and indicators, the voices for instance. Crazy or not, two things were for certain, that she had to take care of Renotta and that they had no other place to go.

She tried to stand but found her legs trembled and her feet tingled... she suddenly realized that she was damp, almost soggy... she had not noticed that she had been sweating but she was soaked to the skin... she changed her nightie and went back to bed.

Wynne awoke the next morning with a new attitude, a new mood and a new perspective...she had seen a sign a few days ago at a storefront not far from the house, advertising a job opening and she decided that she would go and apply first thing Monday...while she's out, she will find some really potent bug bait so that she can get rid of the horse-sized cockroaches, at least get them under control, even if she can't drive them out altogether. From now on, she and Renotta will shower and get dressed for bed much earlier than usual so that there will be no water running after 7 in the evening... they will just have to sit around in their nighties and watch TV until it was time for bed...she would not explain to Renotta the reason for this change in routines...no point in tempting fate or pushing her luck, trying to explain the inexplainable, even if she could...she noticed almost immediately that the churning had ceased in her stomach and that hard burning knot of apprehension had loosen and all but disappeared.

The never-say-die Belle stopped twitching, stood very still and spoke to the few who remained nearby – one too young to hunt, one blind in one eye, one with a foot missing and a female too heavy to be of much use - 'this is not the end... something will happen...someone will forget or get careless and we will again be presented with a banquet...we will dig in and we will survive as we have always done for hundreds of years...we will not give up and we will not go away.' They all gave Belle their best Blattodea standing ovation... being an expert on survival, Belle was absolutely right.

One Leg Dancing

A few months later, Ona Louise sold her house, put enough money in Yanny's account to cover his tuition for the coming semester plus a little bit more...she then packed up, called the movers and moved in with Lom. She is the happiest she has ever been and rarely has any dark moods or fits of depression. Of course, she still misses the ones she has lost but it is as if an invisible power has healed her heart and filled it to near over-flowing.

Wynne and Renotta are still trying to make peace with whatever or whomever is disturbing their sleep but neither has left the house. El Vengador has all but retired but I'm sure he is not so far away and will come to my aid at a moments' notice.

For this I am grateful:

I am grateful for the love of those who love me...

I am grateful for the rain and the rainbows...

I am grateful for those who take the time to read my books...

I am grateful that the politicians cannot control the weather...

Most of all, I am grateful to all of the Angels who give me another opportunity with each new day to fix what I screwed up the day before.

Cee McAdams

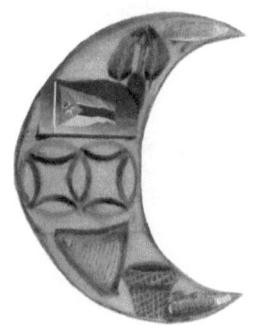